Jump All the Mo

A CHILD'S DAY IN VERSE

Selected and Illustrated by P. K. Roche

PUFFIN BOOKS

PUFFIN BOOKS

Viking Penguin Inc., 40 West 23rd Street, New York, New York 10010, U.S.A.
Penguin Books Ltd, Harmondsworth, Middlesex, England
Penguin Books Australia Ltd, Ringwood, Victoria, Australia
Penguin Books Canada Limited, 2801 John Street, Markham, Ontario, Canada L3R 1B4
Penguin Books (N.Z.) Ltd, 182–190 Wairau Road, Auckland 10, New Zealand

First published by Viking Penguin Inc. 1984
Published in Picture Puffins 1987
Copyright © P. K. Roche, 1984
All rights reserved
Printed in Japan by Dai Nippon Printing Co. Ltd.
Set in Granjon

Grateful acknowledgment is made to the following for permission to reprint copyrighted material:

Harper & Row, Publishers, Inc., and Harold Ober Associates, Inc.: "Bedtime," from *Eleanor Farjeon's Poems for Children,*
J. B. Lippincott Company, copyright 1933, © 1961 by Eleanor Farjeon.

Henry Holt and Company: "How Far?," from *Is Somewhere Always Far Away?,* by Leland B. Jacobs.
Copyright © 1967 by Leland B. Jacobs.

The Literary Trustees of Walter de la Mare and The Society of Authors as their representatives: "Bread and Cherries,"
by Walter de la Mare.

The poems from *Jump All the Morning* can be found in the following books: pages 4 and 16, Robert Louis Stevenson's *A Child's Garden of Verses;* page 6, *Mother Goose's Melodies;* page 7, Christina Rossetti's *Sing-song;* page 8 (left), Kate Greenaway's *Marigold Garden;* pages 8 (right), 10, 11, 14, 15, 18, 20, 22, and 24, *The Oxford Nursery Rhyme Book,* edited by Iona and Peter Opie; page 10 (top right), William Allingham's *Rhymes for the Young Folk;* page 12, Walter de la Mare's *Rhymes and Verses: Collected Poems for Children;* page 21, Laura E. Richards' *Tirra Lirra: Rhymes Old and New;* page 25, *Marguerite de Angeli's Book of Nursery and Mother Goose Rhymes;* page 27, *The Annotated Mother Goose;* pages 28–29, Eleanor Farjeon's *Poems for Children;* page 30, by A. B. Ross *Five Going on Six;* page 32, Leland B. Jacobs' *Is Somewhere Always Far Away?*

Library of Congress Cataloging in Publication Data
Jump all the morning.
(Picture Puffins)
Summary: Poems and traditional nursery rhymes follow two active toys through a busy day.
1. Children's poetry, English. 2. Nursery rhymes. [1. Nursery rhymes. 2. English poetry—Collections. 3. American poetry—Collections] I. Roche, P. K. (Patricia K.)
PR1175.3.J8 1987 821'.008'09282 86-16910 ISBN 0-14-050681-0

Love to Jack

A birdie with a yellow bill
Hopped upon the window sill,
Cocked his shining eye and said:
"Ain't you 'shamed, you sleepyhead?"

One, Two—buckle my shoe;
Three, Four—open the door;
Five, Six—pick up sticks;
Seven, Eight—lay them straight;
Nine, Ten—a good fat hen;
Eleven, Twelve—I hope you're well;
Thirteen, Fourteen—draw the curtain;
Fifteen, Sixteen—the maid's in the kitchen;
Seventeen, Eighteen—she's in waiting;
Nineteen, Twenty—my stomach's empty.

ONE, TWO—
BUCKLE MY SHOE...

NOW I'LL TIE YOUR SHOE...

LET'S EAT...

MIX IT...

STIR IT...

FRY IT...

TOSS IT...

CATCH IT!

Mix a pancake,
Stir a pancake,
  Pop it in the pan;
Fry the pancake,
Toss the pancake,
  Catch it if you can.

Ring-a-ring o' roses,
A pocket full of posies,
A-tishoo! A-tishoo!
We all fall down.

WAIT FOR ME...

MORE...

JUMP HIGHER...

Jump—jump—jump—
Jump over the moon;
Jump all the morning,
And all the noon.

Swing, swing,
Sing, sing,
Here's my throne, and I am a King!

Here am I,
Little Jumping Joan;
When nobody's with me
I'm all alone.

See-saw, Margery Daw,
Jacky shall have a new master;
Jacky shall have but a penny a day,
Because he can't work any faster.

CATCH THAT PIGGY!

Dickery, dickery, dare,
The pig flew up in the air;
The man in brown
Soon brought him down,
Dickery, dickery, dare.

"Cherries, ripe cherries!"
The old woman cried,
In her snowy white apron,
And basket beside;
And the little boys came,
Eyes shining, cheeks red,
To buy bags of cherries
To eat with their bread.

YUM

Cobbler, cobbler, mend my shoe,
Get it done by half past two;
Stitch it up, and stitch it down,
Then I'll give you half a crown.

LITTLE DOG?...

Smiling girls, rosy boys,
Come and buy my little toys;
Monkeys made of gingerbread,
And sugar horses painted red.

Oh where, oh where has my little dog gone?
  Oh where, oh where can he be?
With his ears cut short and his tail cut long,
  Oh where, oh where is he?

15

The rain is raining all around,
It falls on field and tree,
It rains on the umbrellas here,
And on the ships at sea.

RUPERT THE COBBLER

OSCAR'S VERY SMALL BOOK STORE

BETTY ANN'S SWEET SHOPPE

LOST
LITTLE DOG
SHORT EARS
LONG TAIL
REWARD
M.T. TINKER
MOTHER GOOSE LANE

17

ALMOST HOME!

Pat-a-cake, pat-a-cake, baker's man,
Bake me a cake as fast as you can;
Pat it and prick it, and mark it with T,
Put it in the oven for Tommy and me.

RING! RING! RING!

PUSSY CAT IS SICK TODAY...

Who's that ringing at my door bell?

A little pussy cat that isn't very well.

Rub its little nose with a little mutton fat,

That's the best cure for a little pussy cat.

PUT HIM TO BED... AND RUB HIS NOSE...

ALL BETTER NOW?

So let it rain
Tree-toads and frogs,
Muskets and pitchforks,
Kittens and dogs!
Dash away! plash away!
Who is afraid?
Here we go,
The Umbrella Brigade!

NOW LET'S MARCH...
HUP!...2...3...4!

OH, I DO LOVE THE RAIN...

LOOK... A RAINBOW!

Higher than a house,
Higher than a tree;
Oh, whatever can that be?

Bow, wow, wow,
Whose dog art thou?
Little Tom Tinker's dog,
Bow, wow, wow.

24

Hot boiled beans and very good butter,
Ladies and gentlemen, come to supper.

Three times round goes our gallant ship,
And three times round goes she,
Three times round goes our gallant ship,
And sinks to the bottom of the sea.

Five minutes, five minutes more, please!
    Let me stay five minutes more!
Can't I just finish the castle
    I'm building here on the floor?
Can't I just finish the story
    I'm reading here in my book?
Can't I just finish this bead-chain—
    It *almost* is finished, look!

HERE'S THE TOWER...

...AND THE DOGHOUSE!

FOR ME?

Can't I just finish this game, please?
  When a game's once begun
It's a pity never to find out
  Whether you've lost or won.
Can't I just stay five minutes?
  Well, can't I stay just four?
Three minutes, then? Two minutes?
  Can't I stay *one* minute more?

HALF A MINUTE...?

When my brother Tommy
Sleeps in bed with me,
He doubles up
And makes
himself
exactly
like
a
V
And 'cause the bed is not so wide,
A part of him is on my side.

How far is a dream?
  As far as a star
  High in the sky?
How far is a dream?
  At the close of the day
  A dream is just
  A pillow away.